PARTY CROC!
A Folktale from Zimbabwe

Retold by
Margaret Read MacDonald

Illustrated by
Derek Sullivan

Albert Whitman & Company
Chicago, Illinois

On Monday when Zuva went down to fetch water, fish were swirling around in the pool.

"Fish!" said Zuva. "So many fish!
I wish I had something to catch them with."

A crock stuck its big, ugly snout from the pool.
"What will you give me if I catch some fish?"

"Oh my goodness. A CROC!" Zuva cried.
She knew she should never speak to a crocodile, but...

"If you catch some fish, you can come to a party. Lots of good food at our party."

"A PARTY! I'm a PARTY CROC!"

"How many fish do you want?
Two? Three? Four? Five?
When is that party?" called Croc.

"It's Saturday."

"Promise that Croc can come?"

"Sure, Croc, I promise," said Zuva.

She knew a croc couldn't come to the town and he wouldn't know when Saturday came.

But next morning that croc was asking around.

"Hey, mister! What day is today?"

"It's Tuesday."

"I'm going to a party on Saturday! I'm a PARTY CROC!"

Next day...

"Hey, ma'am! What day is this?"

"It's Wednesday, Croc."

"Just Wednesday?
 I'm going to a party on Saturday!
 I'm a PARTY CROC!"

"Mister! What day is this?"

"It's Thursday."

"THURSDAY! When does SATURDAY come?
 I'm going to a party on Saturday!
 I'm a PARTY CROC!"

Meanwhile up in town...
Zuva had handed out fish all around.
She didn't tell where she got them.
She forgot all about that croc.

"Hey, children! What day is today?"

"Friday."

"Will it EVER be Saturday?"

"Sure, Croc. Tomorrow is Saturday."

"Tomorrow is SATURDAY! I'm going to a party TOMORROW!"

Next morning that crocodile was up so early.
He polished his crocodile scales.
He brushed his crocodile teeth.
He jumped out of his pool.

"PARTY TIME!"

Up the path he danced, singing his party-going song.

"Party! Party!
Going to a party!
Party! Party! I'm a PARTY CROC!"

He danced into town and up to Zuva's house.

"Party! Party! Going to a party!

Party! Party! I'm a PARTY CROC!"

"Oh my goodness! You CAME!" gasped Zuva.

"Get in here and hush. Someone might hear!"

But Croc was stomping around and bellowing.

"Okay, okay. Promise you won't holler, and I'll get you some food."

"Croc won't holler."

"Promise!"

"Croc promise."

Zuva ran to the party and grabbed up some food.

She rushed back to her house... but already...

"Party! Party! Going to a party!
Party! Party! I'm a PARTY CROC!"

"Hush! You MUST NOT SING! Someone might hear you!"

She brought another armful of food.

GLUP! GLUP! GLUP! GLUP! GLUP! GLUP!...BUUUURRRP.

"Okay, go back to the river now, Croc."

But that croc was starting in again…

"Party! Party! Going to a party!

Party! Party! I'm a PARTY CROC!"

"Hush! Here's some more food.
Promise you will be quiet!"

"Croc **promise.**"

"Eat and go back to the river."

GLUP! GLUP! GLUP! GLUP! GLUP! GLUP!…BUUUURRRP.

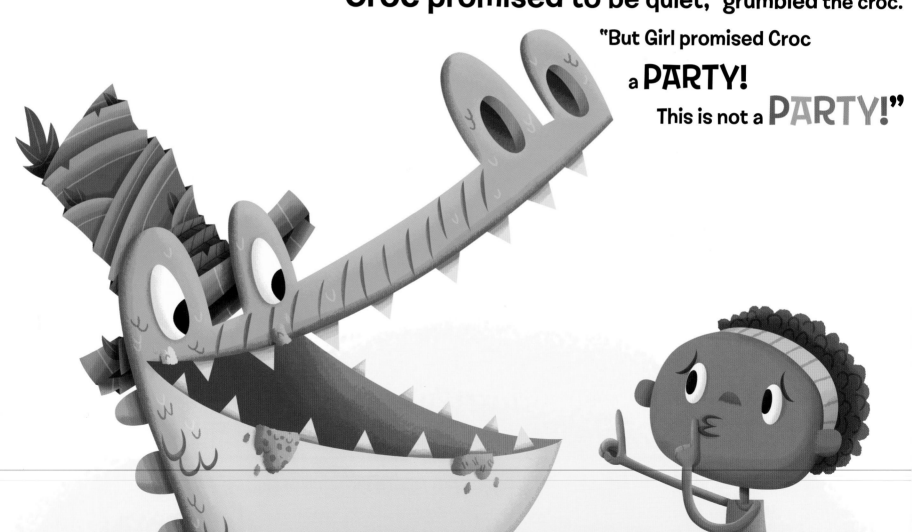

"Party! Party!
Going to a party!
Party! Party! I'm a PARTY CROC!"

"You promised to be QUIET!" shushed Zuva.

"Croc promised to be quiet," grumbled the croc.

"But Girl promised Croc
a PARTY!
This is not a PARTY!"

Croc stomped up the road singing.

"Party! Party! I'm a PARTY CROC!"

There was the party!

Croc crashed right into the middle.

"Party! Party! I'm a PARTY CROC!"

That croc was thrashing around with his tail, knocking people all about.

"WHAT IS A CROCODILE DOING HERE?"

Zuva's father GLARED at that girl.
"What was a crocodile doing in town?"

"Remember those fish I brought home Monday?
The crocodile caught them for me.
I promised he could come to our party,
but I never thought he would come."

"GIRL!" said her father. "Never invite a CROCODILE to a party!
And never make a PROMISE you cannot keep."

All that night no one could sleep up in town.
Because down at the river that crocodile was churning around and around in his pool.

"Party! Party! When's the next party? Party! Party! I'm a PARTY CROC!"

So on Sunday...

"Hey, Croc! Sorry about that promise.
But a PARTY CROC needs a CROCODILE PARTY!"

"Party! Party! Crocodile Party!
Party! Party! I'm a PARTY CROC!"

ABOUT THIS TALE

This story was inspired by *The Lion on the Path and Other African Stories* by Hugh Tracey (London: Routledge and Kegan Paul, 1967). Tracey, an ethnomusicologist (someone who studies music and culture), collected this story from the Karanga, a clan of the Shona people in Zimbabwe. The tale is retold with the permission of ethnomusicologist Andrew Tracey, Hugh's son. You may find music used by the Karanga when telling the story in *The Lion on the Path*, along with the somewhat more boisterous original story, in which the croc is given alcoholic *doro* to drink. Tracey's book also includes a story in which a grandmother is given fish by a singing croc, who ends up eating her!

For Murray Cormac Martin, our own Party Croc!—MRM

To Ariel and Trixie—DS

Library of Congress Cataloging-in-Publication Data
MacDonald, Margaret Read.
Party croc! : a folktale from Zimbabwe / retold by Margaret Read MacDonald ; illustrated by Derek Sullivan.
Summary: "In this retelling of a Shona folktale from Zimbabwe, a girl promises a crocodile he can come to a party in exchange for a favor, but since crocodiles aren't allowed in the village, she doesn't expect she'll have to keep the promise"—Provided by publisher.
1. Folklore—Zimbabwe. 2. Karanga (African people)—Folklore. 3. Shona (African people)—Folklore. 4. Crocodiles—Folklore.
I. Sullivan, Derek, illustrator. II. Title.
PZ8.1.M15924PAR 2015
398.2—DC23   [E] 2014023601

Here comes the
big,
mean
dust bunny!

by Jan THOMAS

BEACH LANE BOOKS
New York London Toronto Sydney

Sitting is fun.

Fun?

He weighs a ton!

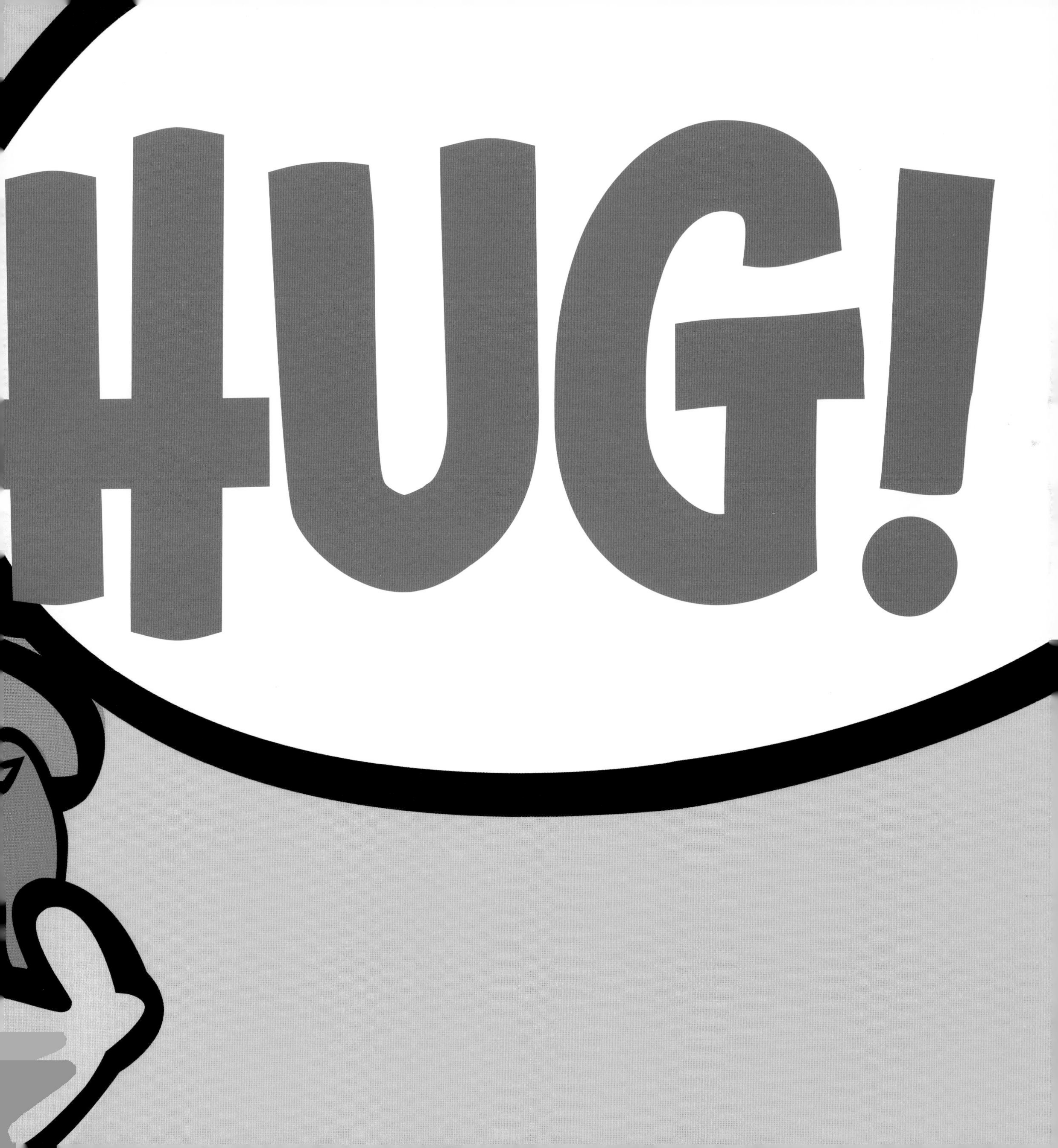
HUG!